Post Box
no.99
AND OTHER STORIES

GW00690028

Post Box no. 99

AND OTHER STORIES

Edited by
Ruskin Bond

Rupa . Co

Published 2005 by
Rupa . Co
7/16, Ansari Road, Daryaganj,
New Delhi 110 002

Sales Centres:

Allahabad Bangalore Chandigarh Chennai
Hyderabad Jaipur Kathmandu
Kolkata Mumbai Pune

Typeset in 11/14 pts. Swiss Light BT by
Nikita Overseas Pvt Ltd,
1410 Chiranjiv Tower,
43 Nehru Place,
New Delhi 110 019

Printed in India by
Gopsons Papers Ltd.,
A-14 Sector 60
Noida-201301

Contents

FOREWORD

Bright young people love to express themselves with the written word. Some do it through the short story, some in verse; others through the personal essay; a few might even try their hand at writing a play.

Creativity can find an outlet through a variety of artistic forms. Writing is probably the most satisfying of all of them; for the written word can be used in many ways.

The best way to be a good writer is to be a good reader. Most successful authors are also book lovers. As children, they soaked up the great literatures of the world. That, and their own talents, turned them into good writers.

The Classmate Young Author Contest is a unique and far-reaching competition designed to discover new talent and encourage our future young authors. The success of the 2003 contest resulted in a surge of interest, with an astonishing number of stories submitted by Class 9 to 12 students from twelve cities nationwide. A panel of several distinguished journalists, writers, editors and teachers sifted through the entries and short-listed the top two stories from each of the participating cities. The National Jury, of which I was a member, then had the pleasure of evaluating the twenty-four short-listed stories and coming up with the top twelve finalists and winners. These talented writers were taken to Mumbai by ITC, where they received their awards. The author of the best story won an exclusive, all-expenses paid trip to London, the literary Mecca of the world. It's over fifty years since I made the pilgrimage to London, the home of Dickens, Thackeray, Fielding, Keats, Dr Johnson, and other great writers. It inspired me to write my first novel. Hopefully it will do the same for Jyoti Iyer, this year's winner, whose story 'Post Box No. 99' displays a rare talent.

This year's contest resulted in a greater variety of themes. Jyoti's story dealt with communal tensions at the time of Partition. Sreerupa Chowdhury wrote an excellent suspense story. Akhila Phadnis gave vent to her imagination and described a day in Paradise. Linda Beatrice's story displayed medical and scientific knowledge. Neena Abhyankar wrote an effective ghost story. Another good ghost story came from Romita Majumdar. Jeevan Austin told a story of family love. Shail J. Deliwala, inspired by Martians, wrote a lively science-fiction piece. Debi Talukdar penned a moving account of a man facing death from a terminal disease. Mohd. Salman's story of aliens showed both skill and imagination. A fine tale of sporting rivalry came from Indrani

Basu. And Shriya Pilgaonkar wrote a philosophical piece about a questioning boy and his grandfather.

I enjoyed all these stories and wish all twelve winners could go to London! But we'll wait for Jyoti to come back and tell us about her trip.

I do think that there are a number of future authors among the winners, the finalists, and some of the other contestants. I'm sure we'll be hearing from them again.

Anyone interested in taking up a writing career should get hold of the Classmate Young Author Toolkit. It's full of helpful information and advice for young writers. It is not for sale, but you can beg, borrow or steal a copy from the ITC Centre in Chennai, whose address is given elsewhere in this book. Even after fifty years of professional writing, I find myself consulting their Toolkit!

Ruskin Bond
Mussoorie
28 March 2005

ABOUT THE CLASSMATE YOUNG AUTHOR CONTEST 2004

This contest is an idea borne out of the need to deliver the proposition of Classmate Notebooks: 'Put the fun back into lessons', to its core audience—students, teachers and schools. It has emerged as a powerful concept gaining support by the day. Classmate Young Author Contest 2004 was the second chapter of this unique event. The event has shown heartening growth in the second year itself.

The Classmate Young Author Contest this year reached over 2000 schools and 40,000 schoolchildren in 12 cities nationally. This was tremendous growth compared to last year's figures of 800 schools and 7,858 children in 8 cities.

Classmate Young Author Contest 2004 remained a four-level contest; the same as the previous year. The first was the school contact round in which participation of the top authors was sought from each school. In the second round, these authors were given an Authorship Workshop at the City Finals. They then wrote their stories, which were entered into the contest. A Central Jury evaluated the stories from all the cities and short-listed the top two for each city and sent the same to Mr Ruskin Bond and his jury for the third round— National Finals, Story Round.

The event gained the support of leading literary personalities of each city, who helped make the City Finals Author Workshop a huge success. It was helped along the way by the support of the schools, parents, teachers and the media.

The National Jury then selected the top twelve from the short-list of twenty-four. These twelve Classmate Young Authors were then brought to Mumbai for the National Finals, Author Round where the National Jury interviewed them. The National Jury comprised Mr Ruskin Bond, Ms Githa Hariharan, Ms Subhadra Sengupta, Ms Meher Marfatia, Ms Reena Puri and Ms Monisha Mukandan.

The National Jury then selected the winner from the twelve contestants and that was Ms Jyoti Iyer from Lucknow. She was crowned the winner in a grand ceremony in Mumbai. Though Ms Iyer was adjudged the winner by the National Jury, ITC Limited believes that all the twelve participants were winners in their own right. Therefore, as a prize that they could treasure all their life as their first published work, this book is being published in association with Rupa & Co.

ITC Limited believes that the idea of the contest could travel much further. Efforts are on to ramp up the contest even beyond the levels reached this year.

There is a wealth of talent in the children in our schools. This talent needs to be discovered, recognised and nurtured. Classmate Young Author Contest is a unique intervention aimed at achieving the same.

ACKNOWLEDGEMENTS

Classmate Young Author Contest exceeded our expectations in terms of the support that it has received over the last two years. In a very short span of time, this contest has managed to reach 2000 schools in twelve cities and has shown amazing growth over the last year.

We believe that it is due to the unstinted support of all our partners in the endeavour. This includes the schools and teachers of the participants whose encouragement really helped the event in reaching far higher levels as compared to the year before. We are highly indebted to them for their support.

We are also thankful to the people who made this event what it is—our esteemed juries at the National Level and the City Final level, Eventus Integrated Management Pvt. Limited, our event managers, Percept Profile, our Public Relations partners, the media and Rupa & Co. publishers, who have agreed to publish this book comprising the stories of the top twelve Classmate Young Authors.

We are especially thankful to Mr Ruskin Bond for graciously volunteering again this year to head the National Jury and edit the book.

We believe that the strength of this contest lies in its idea. The strongest supporters of this idea have been the bright young participants of Classmate Young Author Contest 2004. They merit heartfelt thanks from us for making this event what it is and helping us dream of what it could become in the very near future.

Chand Das,
Chief Executive Officer
Greetings, Gifting and Stationery Business
ITC Limited, Chennai

Akhila Phadnis

Akhila is a fifteen-year-old from Chennai studying in the Besant Arundale Secondary School, a unit of the Kalakshetra Foundation.

To her, writing is a way of sharing her feelings and fantasies with people without directly talking about them. Her story, 'A Day in Paradise', is about the devil spending—or trying to spend—a day in heaven to win a bet with an angel.

Her favourite authors include Enid Blyton, Roald Dahl, J.R.R. Tolkien, L.M. Montgomery, Rex Stout and Agatha Christie. Reading is more than just a habit for her: it is an intrinsic part of her life. When she is not reading she is writing, listening to music or beading. She would like to take up a career that combines teaching and writing.

Her motto is a fragment from Edna St Vincent Millay:

> 'My candle burns at both ends;
> It will not last the night;
> But ah, my foes, and oh, my friends
> It gives a lovely light!'

Akhila was awarded the first runner-up position by the Jury.

A DAY IN PARADISE

Akhila Phadnis (Chennai)

'Hurry up! Come on!' grumbled Lucius. These new entries were taking a mighty long time climbing up the steps to Hell. 'Lazy, that's what today's damned generation is,' he said and then chuckled at his own joke. Finally the face of a man appeared and then his body. He held a squirming bundle in his hands, which Lucius grabbed and threw into a locker marked 'Souls Deep Freeze Storage'. He handed the man a slip of sulphurised paper. 'Come back in ten thousand years. If its still got over three cm. square of white in it, you claim it and jump it to heaven. Paradise see? And—' he stopped suddenly. A booming noise was coming from Lower Hell. That meant only one thing! A second later he was gone, leaving behind only an odour of sulphur, garlic and onions.

'Well! Well! An angel in Hell,' he said gleefully. 'I...I come in peace. I bring a message for Lucius, the Devil.' 'Can't you recognise me when you see me fool? Out, spit it out.'

'Wh-What?' The angel was in a state of uncontrollable anxiety. He knew one sneeze and he would be trapped in Hell till the Devil sneezed. And that, God had said with a smile, 'Will happen only when Hell freezes over.' And the messenger was allergic to onions! Sniffing desperately, he gazed up at the Devil. 'What? What? Your message, you blithering knock-kneed nightgown with wings, that's what.' The angel stumbled over his words in his haste to get them out, 'St. Lauren, former resident of Upper Hell, recently released, has an unresolved argument with you. He challenges you to a bet.'

'What bet? Come on I've got work to do.'

'He...he bets that you can't spent a day in Paradise without getting kicked out. If you win he will agree that you won the argument. If you lose he says you must apologise and release twenty-five souls from Upper and Lower Hell, each.'

'Is that all?' the Devil shouted. 'And what do I have to do to enter Paradise? Oh I know, sprout wings, get a halo, play the harp, blah-blah-blah. Anything else?' 'You must be good, and...and take a bath!' The angel disappeared, managing with a heroic effort to suppress his sneeze till he was well within Heaven.

The next morning, as St. Peter opened his book, a sniff made him look up. The shock of what he saw sent him reeling backwards, 'Lucius! Is that you?' The Devil glared at him from beneath a preposterous halo. Monstrous black wings flapped out above his swishing tail. But none of this shocked St. Peter as much as the fact that, 'You've taken a bath?'

'All right! All right! Stop publicising it,' growled Lucuis grasping an entry card and busting through the pearly gates. 'Remember, three bad deeds and you're out,' came the gatekeeper's voice. Stomping through the highway, Lucius bumped into an angel hurrying past with a shopping bag full of holy tomatoes, blessed cucumber and sanity pizza. The angel immediately rose up into the air and began strumming on his harp. Opening his mouth wide he began a song in a rich deep voice.

'Stop! Stop!' moaned Lucius covering his ears. The angel looked down in surprise. 'It was a prayer of forgiveness,' he said reproachfully. 'I don't need to be forgiven and I forgive you for insulting my ears, so shut up and beat it,' snapped the Devil. The angel smiled softly, 'All is forgiven my son. Do not worry,' and he flew off humming to himself. The devil nearly choked with rage. To be forgiven by an angel! And an upstart of yesterday at that! But he realised that bad moods were considered evil deeds in Heaven, and so, quashing his rage, he strode on down the road.

Nearly two hours passed before he met with a second round of trouble. He was peering over a fence gloomily, watching a man water his flowers, when he sprang back as if stung. 'What in the name of A ...' he took a deep breath. '... God are you sprinkling on these blast ... blessed flowers?'

'Holy water what else?' said the man looking mildly surprised. 'Holy water! Oh no!' and Lucius glanced down at his skin where a blister was already forming. 'Haven't you heard of water conservation! Killing innocent little flowers,' he fumed. 'But they like it!' said the man, shocked. 'Go to Hell,' screamed the Devil as his whole body started throbbing from the drops of Holy water. And then he banged his head against the fence as he realised what he had done! 'Oh no! He's really gone to Hell. And now I have to salvage his soul and send it back here otherwise I'll have tons of sneeze-proof angels flurrying around searching for him.' And then he realised with a further sinking of heart that he had also committed his second evil deed! 'Well, well Lucius. Enjoying yourself?' asked a voice maliciously from behind him. 'Lauren! You ... holy ... saintly ...' But he had run out of words, so he just glared at the smug angel standing in front of him. 'You do know that if I win, you come back to Hell, don't you?' he snarled. 'Don't I just? And I also know how much it pains you to let go of even one soul. Just imagine, fifty souls escaping from Hell, Lucius.' A spasm of pain crossed the Devil's face. He glanced at his chronometer. 'Just three hours more for sunset Lauren.' 'Three hours? Your metre's slow Lucius. There are six hours to go,' and another jolt of panic ripped out the Devil's insides as he remembered that Heaven was three hours behind Hell.

We will not dwell too much on the Devil's anguish. It will suffice to say that the next five hours were the worst in the whole of the Devil's eternity. And then one hour before the deadline, the Devil committed his final evil deed. He was lazing around under a tree, his stomach growling. Brought up on hydrochloric syrup and cyamide chips, the mere thought of ambrosia and nectar nauseated him. He glanced around moodily at the berries that surrounded him. From a distance St. Lauren was singing a song of the triumph of truth over evil. The Devil's blood pressure was rising. And he had'nt had anything to eat. Any minute now, he was going to faint. Glancing across at St. Lauren, who was singing with his eyes closed, he made up his mind. One quick word and the berries had turned into his beloved cyanide chips. But just as he started his meal, bells started ringing and the voice of God rang out throughout the orchard, where he was sitting. 'Oh Lucius,' that was the third and final chance. One more evil deed and you will be banished from Heaven, never to enter again!' The Devil nearly scowled but, remembering that disrespect to God was equal to a hundred evil deeds, restrained himself at the last minute. He was willing to do anything to win back Lauren's soul for Hell. And so, he did what he should have done hours before. He went to sleep. And as the sun set, the bells of destiny tolled throughout Paradise. St. Lauren's soul was lost to Heaven forever.

And then the Devil had his hour of triumph. 'The day is past, Lauren,' he called before turning the entire orchard into a flowing river of hydrochloric syrup. He pushed down the church steeple, tore off as many halos as he could, substituted a guitar in place of his harp, and flew all down the main road, belting out the most outrageous songs he knew. He ... But just as it was better not to dwell on his suffering, so is it wise not to dwell on Heaven's sufferings. Lucius was thrown out and forbidden to ever enter again. The soul of the man he had mistakenly sent to Hell was returned with great anguish, but Lauren's soul entered Hell. And, on seeing the fun he had before he was chucked out, ten angels foolishly bonded their souls to him for a thousand years in the hope of living life to the full.

And so the Devil is back in Hell, God is in his Heaven and all's well with the world.

Debi Talukdar

Debi Talukdar is a sophisticated and mature seventeen-year-old of eclectic interests from National Public School, Bangalore. The only finalist from Bangalore, she enjoys activities like theatre, dancing, swimming and spending time with close friends, apart from reading and writing. For this popular and fun-loving girl, writing is a means for her to express her opinion and personal interpretation of a subject.

When asked about her favourite author, she wastes no time in gushing about Paulo Coelho and his simple yet tremendously inspirational style. Her career plans include acting for the stage and research in Psychology.

Her curiosity to explore the human mind leads her to write stories that dabble with delicate human emotions. Armed with a pleasantly sensitive edge to her writing, her story for the National Finals is metaphorical and deals with an abandoned cancer patient finding the strength within himself to fight his illness, which reflects her conviction that if you have a strong belief in yourself, you can take on anything in the world.

Her favourite words are 'When you really want something, the entire universe conspires to help you achieve it'.

Debi Talukdar was awarded the sixth place in the Classmate Young Author Contest this year.

A BALD MAN'S COMB

Debi Talukdar (Bangalore)

I sat on the edge of my bed, staring blankly into the mirror next to the large and airy balcony. I scrutinised my reflection mercilessly, asking the face staring back at me, why?… Why was life picking on me?

No reply. Obviously.

I looked at the face in the mirror again. The man I saw possessed hollow, sunken eyes filled with bitterness, agony and helplessness. He had sagging skin, which looked almost translucent, and his lips were set in a thin, black line.

He had no hair.

I couldn't believe that man was me. Six months ago I had everything. A high paying and satisfying job, a beautiful family and a fulfilling life. Even hair. Then without warning life decided to take it all away. Life decided to strip my life of all meaning and leave it as a gaping hole.

Ironic. Very ironic.

I thought of my wife. She was beautiful. I'd met her at college. Right then I knew she was 'the one'. She completed me in every way and I used to live each day thanking God because tomorrow would be another day to spend with her. I thought of my daughter. Exquisite thing she was. She had her mother's exotic features and my curly hair. She was three and knew exactly what she wanted from the world.

Thinking about them now is painful.

I was the Creative Director for the advertising firm I used to work for. I was appreciated and well liked. I loved my work. Interacting with people, thinking up new ideas. Busy schedules... Ah! So satisfying.

Now that was also gone.

I cried silently, my face still an expressionless slate. I tried to ignore the pain. But it wouldn't go. The mental pain slowly transformed into a throbbing, hammering pain splitting my head apart. The pain was so bad that I was blacking out constantly. Chemotherapy does that to you.

You see. I suffer from brain cancer.

It's been six months now, and I still haven't come to terms with it. I'd found out quite by accident actually. On my daughter's third birthday. We had gone out for dinner, in the middle of which I had a stroke and passed out. I remember vividly the look of worry and concern on my wife's face when I regained consciousness on the hospital bed. Apparently I had been revived in the nick of time, just before I slipped away into an indefinite coma. A series of scans and tests followed on my weak body, which could barely turn sides on the bed, let alone sit up. A week later it was diagnosed that I had brain cancer and I was in my third stage. I was lucky to have survived the stroke without any severe mental damage or memory loss. My left hand however, was paralysed for life.

My wife was in a state of shock when the doctors told her. I remember her weeping outside my room with my daughter on her lap saying 'Daddy's going to die sweetheart. Daddy is going to die!' It was traumatic for both of them. I remember my daughter holding my bony finger and saying, 'Mummy cries all the time. She says it's because of you. She says nothing will be okay again. She thinks you are bad. She doesn't like you anymore. But I like you badly. I just want you to play with me and not sleep all the time. Can't we go home and play?'

Her innocence and childish intuition never failed to stun me. Because soon after, my wife left me taking our daughter along with her. Couldn't bear to ruin her life because of me, she said. The only real support I had, decided to turn its back on me. A month later I started chemotherapy.

It was the most painful experience of my life.

I thought of my wife every day. How she had seemed so concerned and supportive. How she promised she would stay by me and help me see it through. I still couldn't believe she had walked out on me, leaving me alone. She said my sickness would ruin her future. She decided our daughter should see better days.

I didn't even try and stop her.

A full two months of intense chemotherapy followed. My body had lost its rigidity and strength and I had begun to look like a pale, hollow person. I had called my boss and told him that I would be back at work soon.

Eventually I lost all my hair.

Soon after I was allowed to go home, and live a normal life. What was the point? I knew I was dying anyway. But I went back to work. It was the only thing I had left. Brain cancer couldn't stop me from working.

Apparently it could.

The next month I was sacked. My boss said it was in the best interest of his company and my colleagues.

He wished me all the best and said I was a strong man.

I didn't try and argue.

My colleagues gave me cold stares as I collected my things. They kept a distance as if I were contagious. Then the realisation hit me.

My life was over.

But I had to be strong. For myself.

All the people and things I ever cared about had left me. My wife, my daughter and my job. None of them looked back even once. None of them wanted to stand by me. All of them left me alone. To combat my death.

I went home that night and stood in my balcony. I felt abandoned. I reached into my pocket and pulled out the comb I always kept there—a cheap, small, black, little thing. 'I wont need you anymore,' I said and flung it across the balcony.

I cried all night thinking about how my life had changed in the last two months.

But I had to be strong.

I snap back to the present and realise I haven't batted an eyelid and am still staring at the mirror. Out of the blue I hear the shrill ring of the phone in the living room. I snap out of my trance-like state and go pick it up.

My doctor's voice crackles over the receiver. He says that I have to go to the hospital today for another session of chemo. I wince on the other end and say that I will get there in two hours.

I fall unconscious under the bright mean lights as my treatment ensues. After the session, my monthly progress is checked. I have become sick of hearing the same story. The doctor always says, 'We cannot be definite about when we can stop your sessions. Don't worry, we will get your cancer under control soon.'

But I was in for a shock today.

The doctor came in saying that I will soon be fine. They said that my chemo will be less frequent now since my cancer is under control. They say I will live.

I will live!

I am overjoyed as they see me off saying that I should come back only after six months and not next month. I was a complicated case. But may be life had decided it was being cruel and had contemplated giving its meaning back to me.

I whistled on my way back home. I was surprised I hadn't forgotten how!

That night I lay awake thinking. I was thinking about miracles and God and positive things. I knew why I hadn't succumbed to my cancer. I knew why I hadn't slipped into a coma after my initial stroke.

Because I wanted to live. I never wanted to give up. I was thankful to God. He had given me a second chance.

A month passed by.

I sat at the edge of my bed and stared at myself in the mirror. I scrutinised my reflection.

The man staring back at me smiled. This man had lively, black twinkling eyes. He still had sunken cheeks and sagging tired skin, but the colour in his face was back. Yes, he hadn't looked better in months.

And he had begun to grow hair.

Very little hair, but yes it was unmistakable. It was there all right! The hair was symbiotic of his struggle. It was symbolic of all he had gone through alone. It was symbolic of his fight with cancer and how he had come out victorious.

He ran his fingers through his hair. It was growing in patches and he still looked ill ... but he would get better. He ruffled his hair about, overjoyed that it was growing back.

He would need his comb back now!

I went to the balcony and found the cheap, black comb exactly where I had left it. Untouched. It hadn't moved since the time I had thrown it. I picked it up and gingerly brushed off the dust it had accumulated.

Slowly and tenderly I ran it through my hair. I sat down on my bed again and looked at the comb in my hand.

It was the only thing that hadn't left me during the course of my illness. It was the only thing, even though it had been of no use to me. My wife, daughter and job left me. My life left me, but my comb stayed through it all.

The comb looked back at me. Lifeless and motionless in my hand. It was an omen. My comb had come back to me today. It had come back! May be tomorrow my family would, and the day after, may be my job.

The comb warmed my heart and filled me with joy and more importantly ... hope. Hope ... Hadn't felt that emotion in quite a while. Life would get better from this point on. I just knew it.

I owed it all to a bald man's comb. I then looked up at myself in the mirror … and smiled.

Indrani Basu

'Opportunity is missed by most because it is dressed in overalls and looks like work'—this is what sixteen-year-old Indrani Basu believes in and has found to be true more than once. This student of Spring Dales School, Delhi, described this year's Classmate Young Author Contest as a 'blast', in a nutshell. A classical dancer (trained under two different gurus for five years) this sole finalist from the capital enjoys reading, sampling new cuisines and hanging out with friends.

Growing up in a scholarly atmosphere, with both parents teaching at Delhi University, Indrani likes to read crime fiction, her favourite author being Agatha Christie. Though a Science student, Indrani does not want to become an engineer or a doctor, but would be choosing between journalism and law.

Indrani, who was awarded the tenth place in the contest, wrote her story on the topic 'A Walk In the Clouds'. She describes her story as being about 'a young athlete Cher, who has a recurring nightmare and how she copes with it with the help of her best friend and comfort, Jan'.

A WALK IN THE CLOUDS

INDRANI BASU (DELHI)

Cher was running. The grey sky was overcast with shadows. In the distance, thunder rumbled. Fierce rain slapped against her legs. Strands of wet hair clung to her forehead. Her trainers squelched as they hit the ground. She was running the biggest race of her life. Her breath came in short gasps but the knowledge that she was ahead of everyone else kept her going. As the victory line seemed to draw nearer, her energy seemed to increase. A hundred and fifty yards away, she could already taste victory.

But suddenly, her toe slipped, and her body seemed to give away in an instant. As she fell, she saw the world gaping down at her and the dark skies seemed to mock at her clumsiness. That was her last memory. Then she woke up. She was sweating and shivering at the same time.

Cher Stiller was not a model student. She was average in Math, poor in spelling, sleepy in Social Studies (except while passing notes), and a good student of Science. She was also the star athlete of Mont Ford High and sports captain for two years running. Cher had only one dream: to take part in the Olympics. From the age of seven, she had been practicing running for track. And she was good at it. At just sixteen she was a Nationals' finalist, finishing her race as first runner-up. Despite this passion for athletics, her best friend happened to be Jan Brown, who was probably the best description of the class 'nerd'. Jan hated sports and loved Cher. Cher and Jan had been friends since fourth grade.

On the day of Cher's first sports meet, Jan had been the loudest to cheer for her and the first to hug her when Cher came first. When Jan had topped Science and received the school's prize for 'Scientific Mind of the Year', Cher had arranged a giant surprise party for her. They had nothing in common, but everything to share. They were known as the 'Siamese Twins'.

So when Cher woke up after her nightmare, the first person she described it to was Jan. Jan was her usual ever-sympathetic self and told Cher not to worry about it, that it was only a nightmare, and would not actually happen. But Cher was still worried, for she had realised that there was a possibility that it might happen.

A few days later, Cher had to go for another sports meet. Her coach told her, 'You are our best athlete. Do not worry about the competition; we have full faith in you.' Cher was pretty confident, but the competition was tough. She was up against two of the country's best athletes, and she knew that it would be a hard race.

As they lined up near the starting line, Cher eyed the trainers of her two rivals. One of them had one of the best spikes and looked dangerous. The other one seemed pretty sure of herself too. As the referee started to give the commands, Cher focused on her track ahead. Eyes fixed in the front, she felt her adrenalin rush. Sharp at the whistle, she surged forward, and felt the blood pound as she ran. She had a flawless start—she was right at the front. But within a few seconds into the race she felt someone gaining on her, running with her, passing her. It was the athlete with the fancy trainers. Cher could sense someone else gaining on her as well. In a second, the other runner, who seemed to be very confident, passed her too. In a flash, Cher increased her speed, breathing evenly, and crossed the confident girl. Close to the heels of the girl with her fancy trainers, Cher saw the victory line looming up in front. In a burst of speed, Cher crossed the girl and her fancy shoes. Suddenly she slipped and fell. A sharp pain shot up her ankle and she looked up to see her two rivals cross the finishing line. She had lost. As other runners crossed the line, Cher tried to hobble but could not; her coach had to carry her to the stands. As Jan bandaged Cher's leg, Cher tried to recall what had happened. She had almost won, then she fell, and had not even been able to finish the race. Jan tried to soothe her by saying that it was just one of the many races she had run and would have to run during the course of her life, but to no avail. That night Cher had that nightmare again, and to her, it was a reality. Sports meets came and went, but her paranoia remained. In most meets, she came first, but it did not help her regain that confidence that had been hers once. She ate less, slept less.

Jan was worried about her. Whatever she did, it did not help Cher to become her old self once more. Finally, an idea struck her. Instead of helping Cher ignore the problem, she asked Cher to tackle the problem head on. She asked Cher to imagine slipping during the last leg of the race and then getting up and running again. Cher did that, and it seemed to improve matters a little bit. Cher seemed to become more composed and confident.

Meanwhile, Jan had applied for a science major course in college for undergraduates and received a full scholarship. She attended extra classes in the college after school. She was trying to be a science major while she was still in school, something that was unheard of.

Cher, having won the Nationals that year, was going for the Olympics and she was only seventeen. Though all her coaches were encouraging, they had great doubt in this young girl who had had only just so much of experience at the International level. Cher was undergoing rigorous practice sessions for what would prove to be one of the most challenging races of her life. Jan was absent for her practice meets as she was studying for her college course. She sent frequent messages to Cher which said—'Best of Luck—I wish I was there.'

Finally, on the day of the Olympics, the humungous stadium was packed with sports enthusiasts, and as Cher looked at the crowd, she suddenly missed Jan. As her race drew nearer, she could feel some of her old fear coming back and her mind seemed to swirl with all sorts of sinister possibilities. There was a point when she almost felt like a nervous wreck when her coach handed her a cellphone and said, 'It's Jan.'

With relief washing over her, Cher took the phone and mumbled a hello. Jan just said to her, 'Don't worry, you will win. I have faith in you. And so should you.'

As Cher warmed up for her race, with Jan's words echoing in her head, she thought of nothing but victory. As the referee told them to stand in line, she fixed her eyes to the front. 'Ready.' She put her right leg forward. 'Set.' Her eyes straight ahead, breathing through her nose, she felt a wave of excitement. 'Go.' She was off. Straight as an arrow, faster than the wind. 'This is it,' she said to herself. 'This is the rat race, and I will win it.' The competition was tough but she was tougher. The sky had seemed heavy with clouds, now they opened up and it poured. With water against her face and water slapping her legs, she ran, but déja-vu surrounded her. She was winning, but ... As thunder rumbled, she felt another stab of fear. The finishing line was just ahead, but it was getting muddy. Her competitors were slowly gaining behind her, and as she ran, she felt herself slip, slip, slip away … but then suddenly, as if some invisible force were helping her, she regained her balance to cross the victory line just in time to win, to overcome her fear, to learn to have faith in herself.

As the crowd broke out in thunderous applause, she could see in the distance a figure running wildly towards her. As Jan enveloped her in a hug, she whispered, 'Congratulations! And congratulate me, I am finally going to be a science major.' Cher's only reply was, 'Yes, let's walk on the clouds, they are ours.'

Jeevan Austin

Seventeen-year-old Jeevan from Navanirman Sr. Sec. School, Cochin, immediately strikes you as somewhat different from other boys of his age.

His youthful exuberance is tempered by a sensitivity of nature, which is reflected in the stories penned by him. He is interested in Western history and his motto is to bring out the hidden voices of those suppressed to the fore.

Apart from writing, he enjoys reading, music, surfing the Net and spending time with his friends. His favourite authors include Matthew Reilly, Dan Brown and John Grisham.

His ambition is to be an aeronautical engineer and try to scale heights in his literary career.

Jeevan was awarded the Jury Special Mention Award for his authorship.

A PRECIOUS MEMORY

JEEVAN AUSTIN (COCHIN)

One very quiet and cosy winter evening, I saw grandpa looking out into the sea that stretches out for miles in front of our house. He never usually does that. He normally confines himself to his room downstairs.

I went up to him and asked whether everything was all right and he nodded. I wasn't sure, but felt as if he were trying to hide something from me. I wasn't afraid of grandpa...it's just that I knew so little of him. No one ever talked to him much and he had very few friends, in fact none lived anywhere close to Freibourg. I reached out to put my arm around his shoulders but I couldn't, he was too tall for me and I was hardly eleven years old. To my surprise he grabbed me to his side and hugged me. I can barely remember him hugging my father. Anyway, I was happy...

But still, I knew that not everything was what it seemed at home, and while he was running his fingers through my hair, I asked him, or rather demanded, that he tell me the truth... what I had to know.

Grandpa looked into my eyes and said, 'Well, Ezekiel, I think you are old enough to hear what I'm going to tell you.'

'Your parents and I always wanted the best for you and only prayed that by keeping this family secret you'll be safe. Safe from anyone! Safe from the Germans who want you and me and the rest of our family.'

He began, 'The year was 1939, and Germany was facing hard times both economically as well as politically. But none were suffering as much as we Jews. We were hunted like wild animals. From place to place people who considered us as a sign of bad luck shunned us. Signboards carrying the message "Juden Verboten" (Jews Forbidden) were a common sight all over the country, denying us our rights. We were short of food and other supplies.'

'It's all right, grandpa ... you are safe now,' I told him. But he raised his voice and said, 'No, no ... it's not all right. With half-charred buildings in Berlin, with nobody to rely on, it was not all right!' He went on, 'One October night, there was the usual cries of babies and loud explosions of bombs and exchange of gunfire. The Nazis called it "Kristall nacht", or 'Crystal Night', and planned sudden attacks and mass capturing of Jews who were then sent to various concentration camps. Officers of the regime, with the usual air of pride around them, threw stones at Jewish-owned businesses and houses to humiliate us.

'The time was around one in the morning. While most people are meant to be sleeping, we were scared ... we didn't know what lay ahead of us ... life or death. My father took me in his arms and promised me that he would never leave me ... That's when it happened... "Thud, thud thud", I could hear the officers walking up the staircase to raid the apartment for the Star of David insignia—all the Jews had to wear one on their right arms; I had one, so had everyone in my family. Someone opened the door without knocking, I can still feel the cold air that swept into the room where my father was holding me, half crying ... so cold, so terrifying!

'The officers reached out their arms and said Heil, Hitler. The gravity of the situation hadn't sunk in for me and I tried to imitate him, clutching on to my father with my other hand.'

For a short period, I thought grandpa was smiling, but I was mistaken... He was buried in a pain that he didn't want to reveal to me. A smile that hid a lot of facts, true instances.

Grandpa carried on with what he had to say.

'The officer questioned my father and all that I can remember was that we were forced to flee our apartment. Downstairs, the roads were packed with officers stacking Jews in trucks to be sent to death cells. I was shoved into one of the trucks and before I could even make sense of what was happening, I was separated from my family and on my way to some place I didn't know. I started to cry and shout for help … but all in vain … I had no one to help me. Not even my father!

'Next morning, I found myself in a corridor lying on a floor so cold… so unwelcoming. I didn't think twice but went forward to a counter where a gendarme was taking notes. I asked him where my father was. He on the other hand asked me all my details including my father's name. I boldly replied "Nicholas Hunger". Then, without even taking a look at me, he entered into an office that was full of pictures of leaders including that of Mussolini, Hitler and so on. It also had a wonderful polished mahogany desk in the centre. But otherwise the room seemed pretty plain.

'The officer came out again and told me to wait in the corridor. I listened and sat on one of the many wooden chairs. I waited for hours and hours. People and officers kept going in and out of the building … I thought of my father … he promised me that he would never leave me and now… ? He's a liar, a bare-faced liar, I thought to myself. I hate him … I hate my father.

'Then after nearly six hours of waiting, my father entered the corridor and was led into the office by an officer. From the office, I could hear loud arguments and heated negotiations. Finally my father came out of the office with his hands cuffed behind him. I was shocked. I rushed over to my father but the accompanying officer pushed me away. He looked at me cunningly and said, 'You are lucky, boy, this time! But next comes your chance!'

Grandpa looked at me exhausted and full of grief. He said, 'My father exchanged his life for mine so that I could live and I really don't know what to do now ... whether I should be satisfied, angry or happy that I'm alive today and close to a grandson whom I love a lot.

'This is my most precious memory, when I was shown that everything around you is fake and that there is so much more that adds to living, to your survival—faith, love, family!'

Grandpa stopped talking and just looked out into the sea that stretched for miles ...

Jyoti Iyer

This cheerful sixteen-year-old from Lucknow believes that writing and making music are the best outlets for her creativity. She plays the guitar and the piano whenever she has free time away from her duties as Head Girl of City Montessori School.

Her story, P.O. Box No. 99, set in the Subcontinent in 1947, is a tale of friendship and of nostalgia. It makes the reader believe that true friendship can survive the hardest of times. Jyoti has written other stories about the partition of nations and lives.

She likes the works of Richard Bach, Roald Dahl and J.R.R. Tolkien, and one of her favourite books is Ayn Rand's *The Fountainhead*. As yet undecided about a choice of career, Jyoti hopes for a fun job like advertising, which involves both writing and imagination.

A line which she likes to describe herself with is 'I, a universe of atoms, an atom in the universe.'

She was crowned the Classmate Young Author 2004.

POST BOX NO. 99

JYOTI IYER (LUCKNOW)

11:55. 11:56. The last broadcast of the night was a minute late. Even that one minute sent an arrow of doubt piercing through every heart in the room. The men rose, and almost instinctively went to the large radio set in a corner of the room. As they huddled close to it, the women held each other's hands, in their anxiety even allowing their dupattas to slip from their heads.

Outside, there was a heavy silence. An August night which might have been pleasant a few years before, now felt like the dead of winter, a mist of fear hanging like a waiting shroud over the city of Amritsar.

It was 1947. A year which no Pakistani can ever forget: a year which set brother against brother, drew a border across their land and filled hearts with emotions. So many hearts filled with sadness or regret. In Punjab and across the border in Sind, brothers of old shared a common emotion: hate.

Finally the low hum of the radio became a mess of static. Then a voice said 'Asalaam Walekum' and began to narrate coldly the latest happenings in Lahore, which consisted mostly of Sikhs leveling Musalmans killing Sikhs. The listeners could understand little Urdu but knew the meaning of 'Shaheed huye' and 'mare'. They also knew that one was used to describe the death of a patriot. The second was used to describe just a death. And those commonplace deaths encompassed the value of the lives of so many Sikhs who were still in Lahore, still in Pakistan waiting to die, waiting to be killed.

The listeners sat in silence, their blood boiling and faces grim. But they continued to listen carefully—one word was their reassurance. Every Friday, one word hidden in the broadcast was the confirmation that their kin were safe. And as the announcer rattled off figures of those injured, dead, homeless, separated, they heard it. 'Ninyannave,' the announcer said and coughed. A sigh of relief ran like a current through the dingy room. Ninety-nine and a cough told these Sikhs that their sons, brothers, parents and friends were all safe.

Many kilometres away at a radio station in Lahore, Haji Ayyaz Hussain set his microphone down on the counter and sat with his head buried in his gnarled hands. The very hands which had gripped those of his best friend, Jaspal Singh, many, many years ago, on the day they first met. And Haji Saheb remembered that day with neither nostalgia nor regret nor hatred. All he felt was pain... It was 1883. A nine-year-old boy in a bright red turban stood legs apart, arms akimbo, glaring at his opponent—a dirty looking boy in a kurta pyjama like his own, a cap on his head and a glint in his eye. The turbaned boy yelled in his child's voice—'Get off my land you dirty brat!' Back came the reply. 'This is my land. Ask my Abbu.' He said it calmly but his eyes shot a challenge at the hefty turban-wearing boy who thought the world of himself. In the same instant they shouted 'Pappa' and 'Abbu'. Two farmers suddenly appeared out of the tall sugarcane stalks, laughing. The boys were shocked. But the farmers kept laughing till Randhir Singh said. 'O brother Faizal, our sons don't like each other!' which made them laugh even louder. After a while the other man told the children: We are Randhir Singh and Faizal Hussain, neighbours and friends. And you, our angry sons, will also become friends soon!'

The first time the boys clasped hands, their fathers had had to force them. But the next time they met, and every time after that, they met like the best of friends, which is of course what they became.

Haji Saheb came out of his reverie with no expression on his face. These long years had taught him that emotions only made one weak. He rose without a sound and stepped out of the tiny recording room, but felt no less cloistered even when he reached the gate of the building. He watched the guard lock the doors one by one, and thought of Jaspal all alone in Lahore.

The next morning he was abruptly awoken by a soft but urgent knock on his door—'Haji Saheb, Haji Saheb,' the visitor whispered through the thin door. He quickly got out of bed and went to the door, opening it only a crack. He saw a small boy about seven years old standing at his doorstep. He recognised the boy, but instead of a smile, he greeted the boy with a look of horror. He dropped to his knees and gripped the boy's shoulders so tightly that he yelped with pain. 'What happened boy, what happened?' he asked frantically. The boy only said, 'Let us go in Saheb, first go in then I talk.' As soon as the door was shut the boy began to shake with sobs. It was as if Haji's worst fears were confirmed. 'Insha Allah Jaspal…' he prayed. 'All are gone,' howled the boy. 'All are gone all are gone.'

Haji Hussain's heart almost stopped. His head swam and he regained his balance only just in time to keep from fainting. Full of fear, he said through clenched teeth one word—'Jaspal?' The boy composed himself slowly. 'Only Jaspal Chacha left,' he said in his broken Urdu. 'Saheb will save him?' he pleaded. 'Yes, yes, yes … Saheb will save …' Haji's voice trailed off. It was easier said than done.

Back in Amritsar the younger men were angry. They were saying nasty things like, 'Why was a Musalman trusted!' and 'Yesterday's broadcast was late, tomorrow may be that foul Haji will decide not to help us after all!' And then the elders shouted at them, scolded them and ordered them to keep their mouths shut about things they did not understand.

After all, they knew if there was one man to be trusted in all of the world, they would choose Haji Hussain above their own brothers.

At the General Post Office, Lahore, the morning mail brought with it great hustle and bustle. An old man dressed in the grey of the postal uniform, was pushing a large crate towards the outgoing van. The supervisor shouted, 'Hey what's in the crate? Trying to smuggle something away are you!'

'No, sir,' he fumbled, reaching into his pocket for a slip of paper. He took it out and handed it to the supervisor with a gnarled hand, the other firmly planted on the crate. The note read:

'By the order of the Ambassador of Pakistan to Hindustan:

Kindly ensure that the gentleman who gives you this note is allowed to personally see to the safe delivery of this package to His Excellency, the President of India in New Delhi, via Amritsar. Thanking you,

Haji Ayyaz Hussain'

The address was Post Box 99, Guru Gobind Singh Mohalla, Amritsar, Punjab, India.

By the next evening, Amritsar had regained a lost son by the name of Jaspal, who arrived escorted by his old friend Haji Saheb, although in not too comfortable a fashion, in one piece.

And no one in Lahore knew that P.O. Box 99 was that of the wanted 'criminal' Sikh Jaspal Singh, whose only crime was his presence in Lahore after Partition.

Well, the young boys of Amritsar were calm about the broadcast then. The midnight radio broadcast from Lahore was never heard again, nor was any trace of His Excellency, the Ambassador. And Amritsar gained another son, by the name of Amrit Singh, who lived with his 'brother' Jaspal and received mail at P.O. Box 99 everyday, from Sikhs across the border, everyday transporting large crates, one gnarled hand on the trolley, and the other firmly planted on his package.

L. Linda Beatrice

Linda Beatrice Louis is a student from the portals of St. Dominic's Anglo Indian School, Chennai. Intricate plots, exotic language and human drama are what captivates her; *The Lord of the Rings* and *The Bourne Identity* are her all-time favourites.

She describes writing as a passion and a skill to be mastered and expresses a desire to write stories which are deep and suspenseful, yet intriguing and exciting. No doubt, her role models, J.R.R. Tolkien and Alistair MacLean, inspire her to write a story like 'Ctrl-Alt-Del' in which she beautifully gives life to the characters. Giving it the aura of real time drama, she describes the dilemma which the protagonist faces when she has to decide what is morally right and wrong.

When questioned about her future plans, this sixteen-year-old reveals that her ambition is to become a spokesperson or a news anchor with writing as an alternative career. She believes that

> "Success does not mean the absence of failures,
>   It is the attainment of ultimate objectives.
>   It means winning the war, not every battle"

She follows one rule in life—Don't let go of the happiness and fun of today to slave for the success of far off tomorrow. She adds that 'I may seem to be unlike others, but I'm not different, I am the difference'.

She was awarded the fifth position in the contest.

CTRL-ALT-DEL

L. Linda Beatrice (Chennai)

Scarlette Schneeberg hurried down the corridor, her brown hair flying out behind her. Buttoning up her lab coat she arrived at an electronically sealed door, sliced her identification card through the slot and pressed her hand against the palm analyser. The doors slowly hissed open, revealing a sight that was momentarily blinding to the eyes. Gleaming white tiles covered every inch of the floor, ceiling and walls. Machines fifteen feet high towered above her. Countless panels of computer screens flashed meaningless messages. Dr Schneeberg walked in and made her way to the group of scientists cluttered around a glass case. Inside the case was a revolving three dimensional image of a cell. 'Hey Scarlette,' one scientist called out. 'Regular duty call is at eight 'o clock. It's ten o'clock now.' 'Sorry Matt,' she grinned. 'I slept till nine.' 'Okay. But let me tell you, this cell is really great to work on. I mean the physical variations it shows when certain stimuli are applied to it are exactly similar to that of a real living cell. By working on this, who knows, may be you can try out your research on slowing down ageing and get positive results.'

Scarlette's hand went very still. It was a lifelong dream of hers, to slow down the irreversible process of ageing. 'Are you serious Matt?' she asked. 'Sure I'm serious. This artificial cell serves as a great test subject. Remember that chemical you developed last year, designed to avert the activities of such cells? You can't get an approval without showing that the drug has no toxic side effects.' Scarlette nodded. She knew all this bureaucratic jargon. The drug which she called Lesatovin initiated certain processes in the human body which would stop ageing. Certain hormones were secreted and the secretion of some other hormones were arrested. The end result was that the rate of the cells' activities changed. But Dragens Med, the research firm she worked for did not grant her money to continue the project and also forbade her to use human beings as test subjects. The drug worked well in the case of mice and rabbits, but Scarlette needed to work on human cells. Seeing that this was not possible she had stopped the project. But now with these artificial, computer-generated cells, she could test her invention safely.

'But Matt,' she frowned 'I need a physical cell to work on. This is only a three-dimensional effect.' 'You don't need a real cell, Scarlette. All you have to do is input the various ingredients of your drug in the correct concentrations into the system that controls the cell. You can visually see how a normal cell would react. Whether it shrinks, changes colour, enlarges ... any such change can be observed. So ...' But Scarlette was no longer listening to him. Already she was leafing through her documents and she soon found her papers concerning Lesatovin. Hurrying to the computer she entered the composition of her drug and programmed the system to send the stimuli to the cell. Tense with anticipation she initiated the process by pressing ctrl-alt-del. After some time the computer displayed the biological changes recorded. As she scanned them Scarlette couldn't believe her eyes. The results were exactly what she wanted. Armed with these records, she forced Dragens Med to advance money for the project. And she succeeded. The project was now a reality.

Work began in frenzy. A team of five scientists consisting of Dr Scarlette Schneeberg, Dr Mathew Roland, Dr Eunice Salome, Dr Elma Raphael and Dr Frederick Paltran worked on the project. Lesatovin was developed. All the animal test subjects reacted favourably to the drug. Many symptoms that were usually attributed to ageing like hairfall, weakening of muscles, disintegration of bones, etc. were controlled. Lesatovin became a wonder drug. The scientists only had to prove that human beings reacted the same way. A sixty-year-old convict was chosen as a guinea pig. When Lesatovin was administered, his cells showed a definite change. The scientists were overjoyed. 'This is great!' said Dr Harol Macphase, head of the research department. 'But you need to perform more experiments, try out people with different ailments, find out if the drug cures those ailments too,' he said. Advertisements were inserted in the local paper. For Dr Scarlette Schneeberg it was a dream come true. John Roomer, an old man with advanced diabetes, volunteered for the project. Dr Mathew Roland was a little uneasy about administering the drug to a sick man, but seeing that the old man had volunteered and knowing how enthusiastic Scarlette was, he gave in.

Everything was in readiness. John Roomer had given his full consent for the project. Scarlette, seated at the main computer console, pressed the appropriate keys—ctrl-alt-del. Everyone watched in tense anticipation as the liquid dripped into the tubes attached to his body. For some time nothing happened. And then, barely noticeably, the subject twitched. As minutes ticked away, his twitches grew more pronounced. By the end of fifteen minutes his body was shaking uncontrollably. The flow of Lesatovin was immediately stopped but it was too late. After ten more minutes the aged body went totally still. Dr Elma Raphael, who was standing nearest to him, bent over his heart and then turned back to Scarlette with a pale face. 'He is dead,' she whispered.

The uproar over John Roomer's death was enormous. Subsequent investigations and autopsies conducted by other doctors revealed that he had also had a weak heart. The public decried the scientists as murderers. The matter was taken to court.

Dr Scarlette Schneeberg stood very quietly in the witness box. However, when the district attorney questioned her she looked up proudly. 'We didn't do anything wrong. Our research suggested that using Lesatovin would not have any toxic side effects in the case of diabetes. We didn't know his heart was weak.' 'But Dr Schneerberg is it not routine that a preliminary examination be made of the test subject before you proceed?' 'In normal cases, yes,' she answered. 'But when we went through his medical records, there was nothing to suggest that he had a heart condition. Mr Roomer himself did not give any indication that he had a weak heart. In accordance with his diabetes records, we did test his blood sugar and found that we could inject the drug safely. Only when the subject demands a complete check up do we test all his organs.' 'Putting aside Mr Roomer's heart condition, do you think that you are morally justified in your research?' For the first time Scarlette's tone faltered. 'What do you mean?' she asked. The D.A.'s assistant leaned close, 'Have you thought about the moral correctness of continuing your project? Do you think it is right for you to try to stop ageing, a natural process, which, if you will pardon my religious expression, was ordained by God?' And to that Scarlette had no answer.

She drove home in silence. That day was one of the most embarrassing days of her life. Some people alleged that she was mentally sick and demanded an inquiry into her past. Her friends had been questioned about her and, unwillingly, one of them had spoken about her fear of ageing. Tonight, a week after the hearing in court, she thought about her fear. A fear of becoming old. It had stemmed from her childhood...

Her grandparents were loving and benevolent people, but by the time she was ten years old they were old and infirm. They required a lot of care. Her parents did it without complaining, but she could see that it irked them. Her grandmother's tantrums, her grandfather's need for constant care, she saw it all. Scarlette could see that they did not like being dependent, but they had no other choice. As a child, she could perceive her grandparents' feelings. A feeling of being unwanted. And she had been afraid. Afraid of growing old. Afraid of losing love. That fear had stayed with her throughout her life. It had given her the incentive to find a cure for ageing. And now it had come to this.

Scarlette was tired of the media scrutiny. She was tired of the baleful glares that were cast in her direction. She had still not reached a decision about the project's future. Her colleagues were avoiding her. In order to escape, she applied for a week's leave and went away. She had a small cottage at the foot of some hills. In spring, the valley was really beautiful to look at and it was peaceful. She tried to pull herself together and make a decision about her research. One morning she woke up and walked out to the porch. In the neighbouring cottage there lived an elderly couple whose grandchildren had come to visit them. The lady was on the porch knitting, and even as Scarlette watched, the grandfather come to the house, holding his granddaughters by the hand. The little girls had a handful of flowers each and, giggling in glee, they presented it to their grandmother. Scarlette watched the old couple as they went about their work leisurely. 'How very different from my hectic life,' she reflected. In a moment of poignant insight, she realised that old age had its own privileges. A divine peace came with the advancement of years, along with a philosophical outlook on life. Before she left the valley, she went to church, a small chapel with an old world charm about it. Kneeling down, she prayed for forgiveness. She realised that science was to be used for curing illnesses, but not to defy God, nor try to stop what must naturally, inevitably take place.

When Dr Scarlette Schneeberg M.D. returned to her hometown she found that the uproar had died down to a certain extent. She went and apologised to the family members of Mr John Roomer. The next day she submitted a document in court announcing that she was discontinuing her work on Lesatovin, amazing her colleagues. But the Board of Directors of Dragens Med weren't quite so pleased. Scarlette was summoned and questioned as to why she had decided to stop her research. 'The people arent quite so opposed to Lesatovin now. Once you remove its toxic effects and get it approved it will be a wonder drug. Everyone will buy it. You and Dragens Med will be famous,' they said. But Scarlette was firm. 'It does not matter whether public sentiment changes or not, I feel that it is wrong and that is my last last word.' Walking out she marched to the lab. She opened all her files concerning Lesatovin and then, taking a deep breath, she pressed some keys on her computer, terminating the process. She pressed Ctrl. Alt. Del.

Neena Abhyankar

Neena Abhyankar is a fifteen-year-old living in Pune. She likes reading, listening to music, surfing the net and is addicted to chocolate. She hates vegetables, but unfortunately has to eat them!

To Neena, writing is a way to express what she thinks or feels so that other people know what she is thinking.

Neena's story is a sort of ghost story, involving a bet and a "haunted" house but to know more she suggests that you read the story yourself !

Neena is a voracious reader and will read anything that interests her, but her select favourites are books written by P. G. Wodehouse, J.K. Rowling and Agatha Christie.

Though Neena hasn't planned ahead, her short-term goal is to pass her upcoming board exams with good marks! Long-term, she wants to study either Psychology or journalism.

Neena Abhyankar was given the Jury Special Mention Award.

THE LAST LAUGH

Neena Abhyankar (Pune)

Natasha Malhotra watched as her twin brother, Karan, dived off the board into the deep end of pool. Splash! Water flew all over her, completely drenching her. She screamed. 'Karan! Why can't you jump carefully? You are ruining my tan!' she yelled at him. Karan just grinned and swam across the pool to join his best friend, Rohit.

Rohit and his sister Anushka were the twins' neighbours. The four of them had bonded at their first meeting when the Malhotras moved there six months ago, more so because Rohit and Anushka were twins too.

Now, Anushka laughed and turned to her friend. 'Forget it, Nats, boys will be boys, you know. Forget it. Tell me, did you read about the house on Karnik Road? They are tearing it down next week.'

Rohit and Karan climbed out of the pool and flopped down beside the girls. 'Isn't that the house everyone says is haunted?' Karan asked, drying himself off.

'That's just rubbish,' Rohit answered. 'Nobody has lived there for about fifty years, and it's looking a bit scary with the overgrown garden and everything, so people think it's haunted. They even cooked up a story to support their "ghost".'

Natasha leaned forward, intrigued. 'What kind of story?'

Rohit looked over at Anushka. 'You want to tell her, or should I? Frankly, I'm sick of hearing it, every time the topic comes up.' Anushka smiled. 'Okay, I'll tell her.'

She turned to Natasha with a serious look on her face. 'The story starts in 1920. The house belonged to a British Colonel, Sir George Cartwright. The Colonel had a handsome son called James. James was the most eligible bachelor of his time. Rich and good looking, girls practically swooned every time he looked at them. Now, among these girls was Marjorie Roberts, the daughter of Sir George's best friend. She fell in love with him the first time she met him, but sadly he did not reciprocate her feelings. She pursued him for a year, until finally her reserves broke and she want insane with rage!

'One night, she entered James' room. James was in bed, reading, when she came in. She entered calmly, and closed the door behind her.

'An hour later, Sir George and his wife heard loud screams coming from James' room. The screams were horrible. They rushed to his room and opened his door to see a most horrifying sight.

'James was lying on the ground, blood was everywhere and over him stood Marjorie, her hair a complete mess, dagger raised, a maniacal gleam in her eyes. She was laughing, laughing insane, cackling laughter that chilled them to the bone. Then she stabbed herself.'

Natasha recoiled in horror. Anushka smiled grimly and continued.

'The Colonel and his family moved immediately, a week after their son's death. It is said that they were driven out, driven out by insane laughter that echoed through the halls, any time any one dared to pass James' room. It is said Marjorie still lives in the house, unable to rest, laughing ceaselessly,' Anuskha finished.

Natasha gasped in horror. 'That's terrible!' she said. Karan, however, looked bored. 'I don't believe it. It sounds like every ghost movie we have ever seen.' Anushka glared at him. 'Oh really? So you're that sure, are you? Well let's see you prove it then.'

Karan shrugged. Rohit glared back at Anushka. 'Fine. We accept your challenge. Tell you what, we'll spend a night in that old house. Then in the morning, you can eat humble pie when we succeed.'

Before Karan could say anything, Anushka replied, 'All right then, but if you come back before seven 'o clock, we win. Right, Nats?'

Natasha smiled sweetly at her brother. 'Right.'

So a bet was made. The two boys were to spend that night at the old house.

After dinner that night, the boys set off. Their parents had reluctantly agreed, though the boys were commanded to call home every hour until they fell asleep.

The moment they reached the house they began to have their first doubts.

The house was tall and imposing. Gnarled trees, long weeds and vines made up the garden. You expected lightning and a thunder bolt behind the house.

Inside it wasn't much better. Every room was dusty, dank, dark, cold, uninviting. There was no satisfactory place to put their sleeping bags. Finally, the duo decided to explore the second floor.

They went up the staircase slowly, unconsciously cautious. Years of neglect had made it creepy. As soon as they stepped onto the second floor, they heard a loud sound, echoing though the dark corridors. Instantly both dropped their flashlights and yelled. It had sounded like a peal of laughter. Insane, cackling laughter. Karan looked at Rohit, his face pale. Rohit picked up his flashlight and, handing Karan his, said, 'That was probably the wind.' He seemed to be trying his hardest to keep his voice steady.

They both advanced, slower than before. They opened the first door. The room was empty. A thick carpet of dust covered the floor and everything else. They decided to look further.

As they opened the door of the second room they heard laughter again, except this time it sounded as if it was coming from inside the room. They entered and saw ... nothing.

Nevertheless, they decided to go on. Just as they were about to open the third door they felt a chill going down their spines and they heard footsteps approaching from behind them.

Almost as if trying not to, they turned ... and saw a girl coming towards them. They opened their mouths to scream, but were incapable of making a sound.

The girl passed by them as though she hadn't seen them and went into the room—through the unopened door. The boys stared at it, speechless. Then just as they were about to leave, the door sprang open on its own, throwing them against the wall. They looked inside and saw Marjorie Roberts. Her hair was loose and matted, her hands held a long dagger, her eyes burned with a maniacal fire. Her face was twisted in a hideous grin and she was laughing, laughing insane, cackling laughter.

Rohit and Karan didn't stay. They ran out of the house as fast as their legs would take them.

When they reached Karan's place, where Anushka was staying for the night, they banged on the door begging to be let in.

Predictably, neither of the girls looked surprised.

They looked positively happy.

When the boys had calmed down, the girls explained—'It wasn't real. What you saw wasn't real. It was just special effects.'

The boys stared at them dumbfounded.

Natasha explained, 'You see, Anushka had already told me the story before. We had a bet on with Ruchi Shah that we couldn't scare you two within twenty-four hours. The ghost, the screams, that was all fake. We got Ruchi to have her father set up the equipment which he borrowed from Mr Shah's special effects studio. You do know that he owns the special effects studio downtown, don't you?'

For the umpteenth time that evening, the boys didn't know what to say. Finally Rohit spoke up.

'So, this was all a set-up? Fake? A hoax?'

Anushka smiled serenely, 'Yes, dear brother. But we won both bets, didn't we?'

'No, you didn't,' Karan retorted. 'Your "ghost" was fake, which means that there is no real ghost. Therefore we have won. Our aim was to prove that the story was not true. We have done that. So we have won.'

Anushka retaliated by pointing out that they had stayed at the house for only an hour, which had been the basis of their bet in the first place, thereby proving that the girls had won.

The two of them looked all set to argue the finer points of the bet when the phone rang.

It was Ruchi. Natasha put the phone on speaker mode so all of them could hear.

'Hey guys, listen, I know I promised to make dad set up the speaker and stuff for your bet, but dad needed them for some shot. I'm sorry. But, hey, may be the guys will be scared anyway. I have to go now. See you tomorrow. Tell me about the bet, won't you?' And she hung up.

The four of them looked at each other and rushed to the window, from where they could see the old house.

Was it just their imagination, or did they hear Marjorie Robert's last laugh coming from the old house?

Romita Majumdar

Fourteen-year-old Romita from St. Andrews High School, Pune was the youngest contestant at the Classmate Young Author Contest 2004. She was awarded the eighth position in the contest.

'How a life threatening disaster can help bridge the gaps between people', 'anything unexplainable or supernatural' are some of her favourite storylines. She loves reading short stories. Isaac Asimov, Satyajit Ray, E.A. Poe are among her favourite authors. She also loves to read Jules Verne, Shakespeare and J.K. Rowling, as well as ghost stories. She enjoys observing people.

Her career options are as yet undecided but she has her sights set on the communication and designing field.

Her favourite lines are, 'Have you ever felt like a nobody/ just a tiny speck of air/when everyone's around you and you are just not there.' She loves making new friends.

THE BEGGAR'S COAT

Romita Majumdar (Mumbai)

I didn't believe in ghosts. I didn't believe in vampires nor in fairies and goblins. The word 'supernatural' didn't exist in my dictionary. Neither an atheist, nor an ascetic, whatever faith I had in God was solely to save my ears from mum's complaints. So, that was the only reason I didn't argue with mom when she announced her grand plan—she wanted to visit some fantastic church in Goa which housed some poor saint's coffin. Why can't we let the dead live in peace? And mom—didn't she break enough coconuts to start a flood at the temples already, that she had to start annoying the saints? That too of some other religion. Anyway, all packed we set off.

Now, I won't say that it was bad, but travelling 3000 kms from one part of the country to another just to see a corpse isn't exactly my idea of fun. So instead of staying in the church I went out for a stroll in the adjoining garden. The garden was quite beautiful I must say, but somehow I was still longing to run away to the beach for a swim. As I was enjoying this wonderful moment of tranquillity, lost in the blue sea, I heard a harsh cry jolting me back to reality. I turned around to find an old man—above sixty for sure, wispy grey hair, a coarse and frayed cloak and a face so battered and wrinkled that without the I-am-hungry cry I'd have mistaken him for an oversized walnut. Beggars! The biggest problem of our country. Normally I'd have ignored him and walked away, but something about those crinkly beetle-black eyes made me reach into my pocket. As I handed him a coin he looked at me strangely—as though he could read my mind. I did not like it. I spied my father at the entrance of the church and walked away to meet him. Within minutes I had forgotten the beggar.

Early the next morning I looked out of the window. Just as I had started enjoying the sunrise and calm blue sea, I noticed him standing at the gate. I thought maybe he had a twin brother, or maybe I was just getting stupid. Yet as I said these words I could almost feel that he could see right through the dark glass separating us. For God-only-knows what reason I didn't join my parents on the trip that day and decided to stay in the hotel. Meanwhile, the tramp seemed to have disappeared. Lost in thought, I turned around to drink the tea that the maid had just left. But as I reached for the cup I noticed something very strange—was it just my imagination, or was the cup actually vibrating? Suddenly it tipped over and crashed on the floor. Rooted to my spot, I watched with horror as the bed slid sideways straight towards me.

I jumped away just in time to hear the glass behind me blow into smithereens. Oh my God! An earthquake! I thought. I opened the door and started sprinting down the corridor towards the lift. It was open. As I felt the floor give away, I jumped and slammed the door shut. Suddenly everything became still. As if the earth had been waiting for me to do just this. Breathing a deep sigh of relief I turned around to see two people in front of me. A young lady, who I noticed was pregnant, and—believe it or not—the beggar. 'Phew, I suppose it's all over now,' said the lady. Her eyes were bloodshot.

'Yeah, let's move out,' I answered reaching for the button that would open the lift doors. The door didn't budge. I pushed the button again—no result, except that the overhead light went out with a blast. All right—I'm stuck in an elevator with two people and I don't like it because it is dark. I told you that ghosts didn't scare me—but this did. I was claustrophobic. The young woman seemed to have sensed my fear because presently she was pumping my hand, 'Don't worry, someone will get us out. By the way I'm Mira,' she said. I was too scared to reply. Even in the darkness I could sense him staring at me.

'Whatever happens, happens for good,' he said in a harsh tone. Good my foot—if my throat hadn't been dry I would have been screaming by now. I tried to reach the overhead ventilator by jumping but he pushed me away. How long we stayed in there I have no idea, but with every passing minute the beggar was getting more and more annoying. After a few minutes he pulled out some bananas (two rotten ones precisely) and handed them to us. It had been nine hours since I had last eaten, but fear and tension held me back. I was waiting for something to give me hope, but it didn't come. Once or twice we felt some tremors. Mira tried talking but it was no help. The only thought in my head was, what if no one found us or it got too late. Meanwhile I was trying to keep as far away from the beggar as possible. At last we heard the sound of people walking around, crying out for those lost. I jumped up, 'We're here, can you hear us! Get us out of here!' I shouted, but in vain. Mira also seemed to be getting weaker. As the voices started, I screamed until my lungs felt they would burst although I knew they couldn't hear.

All of a sudden, as if electrified, the beggar jumped up. He pulled off his smelly coat. My first thought was that he was insane, but then he bundled it up and banged it against the wall. As a few coins fell from the pocket, I suddenly realised how years of patience had given this result—the coat was overflowing with coins. Although the loud jangling irritated me, I joined him in hitting the wall. Just when I had lost hope, I heard it. Someone was hitting the door from the other side. As the rays of light streamed in, I felt my knees give way.

When I opened my eyes I was lying in a bed in a tent. I saw Mira in the bed next to mine. I walked out to find the beggar, but in vain. I asked every one I met. No one—not a single soul had seen him. Not even the men who rescued us. But yes they did find in the elevator, other than the two of us, one big smelly coat with pockets full of coins. No one believed me or Mira, because no one saw him. Yet I know that he was there. The beggar and his coat.

Mohd. Salman

Seventeen-year-old Mohammed Salman hails from the city of the Nawabs—Lucknow. A student of City Montessori School, Salman strongly believes in self belief! He cannot accept a lack of confidence in people. He enjoys putting pen to paper, or should it be finger to the keyboard? Quizzing, watching television, cycling (given his leaning towards writing though, you can expect a tour de force rather than a victory in Tour de France!), reading Sir Conan Doyle's celebrated Sherlock Holmes series and J.R.R. Tolkein are hobbies. TV journalism is a career wish and Lucknow is his favourite city. Asked for his take on life, Salman says 'think positive, take confident decisions and believe totally in yourself'. For this Lucknowi, making friends is very important, as is writing. 'It makes me enjoy myself.'

He was awarded the third runner-up position in the contest.

MY DOG AN ALIEN

MOHD. SALMAN (LUCKNOW)

On my sixteenth birthday my father presented me with a white mastiff puppy. I named the pup Fang. As the days passed by, I grew more attached to my pet. At the end of one year, Fang had grown up to full size. An adult mastiff is a very huge animal for a pet, an absolute powerhouse of an animal. This power helped Fang when we used to go on walks, for he used to force me to turn whenever he felt like flirting with a pretty bitch. In a nutshell, it was quite a normal owner-dog relationship. It was quite a shock for me, therefore, when one day my dog began to show some very unusual characteristics.

We had returned from a morning walk and I was preparing to go to school. With a sudden howl of pain, Fang turned turtle and started writhing. The sight was unbearable.

'Fang! Fang! Get up, boy! Get up!' I shouted, in my vain attempts to resuscitate him.

Suddenly the dog stopped writhing and the doors and windows of my room shut on their own. A whirlwind blew through the room. My books and papers whirled in the air. With a blinding flash Fang's body disappeared and in its place stood a tall, anthropoid creature, unlike any that I had ever seen.

The creature was seven feet tall, and had a lean, strong looking 'human body' enrobed in smooth blue skin. The head was bald, the eyes completely white and a smooth patch of skin lay in the region where we normally have a nose.

I was shell shocked. 'Who are you?' I asked, trembling.

'Don't worry, Salman,' was the reply that came from the creature. Its voice had a certain 'electronic' feel to it, akin to the voices of robots in science fiction films.

'I am, what you earthlings call, "an alien",' said the creature with something like a smile playing about its lips.

'I am Zorf, a resident of the planet Atria, distant sixty-seven light years from earth. The story of my arrival on the earth is a peculiar one, but I shall disclose all of it to you, as we happen to be best friends, are we not?' the alien said.

'Yes,' I replied.

'All right then. Now listen carefully. In my planet, Atria, we are all under one ruler. His name is Gromil, and he was elected by the inhabitants of our planet. In our planet, the ruler is chosen by a complicated process. Candidates are chosen by the inhabitants, and are sent to different planets for a sort of training for a period of sixteen Earth years. At the end of this period, we are sent a message after which we get out of our acquired bodies and return home. At home, our ruler arranges a sort of competition, and the title of Ruler Supreme is awarded to the victor, who continues to be the ruler for a period approximating 100 Earth years.

'You might want to know how I spent my "training period" on Earth. As a rule, the three selected candidates have to enter the bodies of dead creatures or objects and learn various skills of self-sustenance and self-defence. I spent the first ten years of my training period as a milestone on the Express Highway No. 66, USA, where I learnt various languages by listening to the people who went by me. The next five years were spent as a tree on one of the northern slopes of Mount Blanc, and the last year was spent with you.'

'But what are you going to do now?' I asked.

'I am supposed to reach Atria in the next fifteen days, and if you like, you can accompany me.' 'Of course!' I shouted, gleefully. But in a moment my happiness disappeared. 'What if my parents come to know?' I asked.

'Now don't worry about that, Salman,' Zorf said. 'I am one of the most powerful people on my planet and I know how to get you out of your problem. You see, I shall freeze time here on Earth by stopping its rotation. We'll go together to Atria, and you can return after the competition. Since no time will have elapsed on Earth in the process, you don't have to worry at all.'

Pleased at this prospect, I consented and went to my wardrobe to pack a few clothes and my camera. Then I and Zorf went out onto the street. He clapped his hands and all of a sudden everything became still. Then he took a device like a torch from inside a bag he was carrying. The device, when switched on, projected forth a black hole in the air. Grabbing me by the wrist, Zorf motioned me to jump along with him and I did the needful.

Swiring and twisting in mid air, we fell into the depths of a dark abyss. I closed my eyes and clenched my teeth to prevent myself from screaming.

When I opened my eyes I was shocked to find myself in a huge hall, painted purple from floor to ceiling, decorated with portraits of famous Atrians. They spoke in French so I could understand them.

'I hope you like this vision. You are right now in the great hall beyond which lies the court of the Ruler Supreme, Gromil. Let us go to the court without any more delay,' Zorf said.

The court was more magnificent than any building I had thought of, even in my wildest dreams.

Huge golden pillars towered up to support the 100 foot-high ceiling. At a 100 yards from the entrance, was a huge red throne on which sat a roly-poly Atrian who, I assumed, was Gromil, the Ruler Supreme of Atria.

'We have been informed of your arrival and of your Earthling guest, Zorf,' said Gromil. 'We welcome our guest and I urge you, Zorf, to prepare for the contest, which shall take place when the Roaring Dwarf Sun rises next morning. For your information, Earthling, I would like to tell you that our planet has nine suns, of which the Roaring Dwarf is the most revered.'

'But, Sire, what is the contest?' Zorf asked anxiously.

'Well, it is a tough one, and is brutal as well, I am afraid. At the beginning of the contest, a Cage of Wit shall be implanted in each candidate's head. The Cage of Wit is a powerful magical instrument, which has the property of translating the most powerful monster in your imagination to reality. These monsters shall duel with each other and the one who kills the other two shall win. There is a difficult condition, however. If you lose, your cage will explode and your head will burst into pieces. In the event of any mishap occurring to you, I shall take the Earthling home.'

The next day the Ruler Supreme took me to a huge open space behind Black Mountain, Atria's highest peak. A huge crowd had assembled around the land where the contest was to take place. Gromil seated me beside him, and ordered for the proceedings to begin.

The officials of the court implanted the magical Cage of Wit into the brain of the contestants. The other two contestants were Vesh, a huge, muscular Atrian, and Aureus, a tiny, furtive-looking creature.

The three candidates assembled in the centre of the open field. A bell was sounded and the contest began. A deafening explosion took place. Vesh had projected his monster. It was a huge, seven-headed black panther. One hundred feet in height and three hundred feet in length.

Another explosion occurred. Aureus' monster had been projected. It was a 500-foot long cobra around whose body thousands of swords revolved. The crowd cheered in anticipation of a close fight. But where was Zorf? He had hidden behind a large rock. A number of people laughed at him. But then all eyes were riveted to the duel between Aureus and Vesh.

The panther clawed and tried to bite the cobra, but injured itself due to the swords revolving around the snake's body. In a swift attack, the snake wound itself about the panther's body. The swords burst in and out of the panther's neck and stomach. The seven-headed panther collapsed and died. Vesh had lost. He fell, weeping out of dejection. A burst was heard and Vesh's head lay in pieces.

Aureus raised his hands in triumph, believing he had won the contest.

'The fight's not over yet,' spoke a calm voice.

Aureus turned around to face Zorf.

'And where is your monster, Mr Zorf?' Aureus asked. 'It's on its way,' Zorf answered. 'A present from Earth.'

He clapped his hands to the sky. A huge black thunder cloud arose in the sky. A thunderbolt hit the ground a few feet from Aureus' snake.

'This is my monster,' Zorf said.

Frightened for its life, the snake slithered across the field, attempting to escape the thundercloud. The bolts of thunder followed it and drove it to the top of Black Mountain. A huge thunderbolt hit the mountain. The entire area was enveloped in a cloud of dust. When the dust cleared, the people saw that in place of Black Mountain stood a pile of rubble. The swords gleaming through the rubble indicated that Aureus' monster had been killed. Another explosion occurred and Aureus' head lay in pieces.

Gromil walked up to Zorf and gave him his coronet, thus awarding to him the title of Ruler Supreme.

'The duel was to be fought using the Cage of Wit,' Zorf said, 'and one thing I have learnt on Earth is that the best way to win a battle of wits, is to cut off all your opponent's means of escape.'

I went to Zorf and congratulated him.

'Thank you, Salman!' Zorf said. 'And now I guess you should go back home.'

He tapped me on the shoulder and said, 'Goodbye! It was a pleasure, being your pet and friend.'

In the next instant, I found myself in my room.

'My dog an alien?' I thought. 'That was fantastic!'

Shail J. Deliwala

For Shail J. Deliwala, the fifteen-year-old Std X student of H.B. Kapadia New High School, Ahmedabad, writing means to pour out his innermost emotions. No one can sit to write, it must come from the inside, says Shail. 'I like to write about nature, inspiring poems (he has a good forty poems under his little belt already!) to spread love for animals, poems on human emotions (mostly on love, anger etc.), stories on pets and stories related to scientific facts which are based on true scientific principles and axioms: stories that are called science fiction.' And in addition to some conventional hobbies, Shail has some off-beat ones too. Like walking on empty streets on a heavenly night! Shail's motto? 'To reach the summit of whichever line I go into' and in his case it is to be a lawyer at where else but the International Court of Justice, UNO.

He was awaded the ninth position in the contest.

WHEN THE MARTIANS LANDED

Shail J. Deliwala (Ahmedabad)

It was in the dead of night that Mr Forsythe H. Brown was testing his new radio-photographic telescope, with a team of astro-physicists. Mr Brown and his team were trying to examine the exact intensity of the X-rays emitted by the cluster of stars UR 13 revolving around a massive black hole located just outside the Milky Way.

As the Gemini Galactra observatory plunged into the mid of midnight, Mr Brown noticed an astonishing sight. High intensity radio waves from relatively nearby sources! Brown's teammate Mr Watson quickly focused the radio photographic lens within the range of the solar system. The photograph showed a very bright object emitting extremely high frequency radio waves so intense, that the radio photographic plate of the telescope automatically got switched off. Mr Brown was shocked. What was happening in the solar system? He had to find out. Using a high power photon laser beam camera, he tried to take a photograph of the object in space, but he couldn't because the object was travelling almost at the speed of light! So, according to special relativity, time would go slower for it. Before Brown or Watson or anyone else could do anything, the lights of the American observatory went out. Something like vapour seemed to fill the room. An eerie silence filled the air, and so silent was that silence, that it resembled vacuum!

The silence was unexpectedly and suddenly broken by a very high pitched siren that rung in the ears of the scientists. The object in space was landing somewhere near the observatory, emitting flashes of blue from what appeared to be laser beams. The air was filled with the blue light. Everyone in the observatory seemed to have been knocked out.

When the sound of breaking glass echoed in the observatory dome where Brown, Watson and the others were working, it was Brown who recovered first. He squinted for a sight of what was going on.

'Get up, gentlemen! Hey Watson get up! Larry, Evans, George! Up my friends! I think I heard a noise. Let's go downstairs for a cup of coffee. I think all we had was a hallucination! So,' said Brown, shaking his head merrily though he was shaken, 'let's go on. Buck up now, we have got work to do after the break!'

All of them, rather pale in the face, trudged downstairs. But an astonishing sight met them—the most extraordinary creatures they had ever seen! The hall downstairs was filled with creatures with sickly green bodies and glistening skin, like that of a vampire's. They had no head but six arms that stuck out at odd angles from their bodies. They had just one leg standing out like a large pillar below their body. Occasionally green eyes without pupils popped out from the top of their bodies. There were about twenty of them, each about two feet tall.

Behind them, Brown and the others could see a massive pyramid glowing blue and green alternatively, and emitting sparks from the apex. Brown was sure he was dreaming and pinched himself hard: it was painful—it wasn't a dream.

'Hey what's going on? Who're you and who permitted you to break into the observatory?' asked Watson bravely.

A loud screeching issued from the creatures. Brown pressed his fingers to his ears and turned on a brand new universal translator lying in a bullet-proof glass case in one corner of the hall.

'We, the men of Mars,' said the voices through the translator, 'urge for protection to be given to us against our evil Chief General Maradonio! Yo, earthen creatures, show your love to us by giving us refuge, as we've escaped Mars to live on the only life-supporting planet, Earth. Sob, Sob, Sob!'

'Hey you can't be Martians! Mars doesn't support such complex forms of life as you,' yelled Watson, angrily.

More screeching issued from the creatures. 'Test our DNA. We are human beings who went to Mars 20,000 years ago to escape the atrocities of the king at that time. We maketh co-operation to you and in turn urge for co-operation from you.'

And the creatures together narrated how the heartless Martian king had used extreme, and highly energised, hard 'Y rays' to convert the human beings to ugly creatures. The Martians told Watson and the others that it was very possible to increase the velocity of light over 300,000 kilometres by using hyper energetic Y-ray particle accelerators in an ultra vacuum medium. These overspeed light rays combined with Y-rays—Y-rays are a mixture of X-rays with tachmesons energised to 5.6×10 NeV—could change the bio-chemistry of a living cell, and this could get transferred to the other cells and change the entire body structure mentally and physically.

'That's it: hold an emergency meeting of the Security Council to help these creatures Brown,' said Watson. At that moment, a phone rang from the end of the hall. 'It's Jim. He says we'd better ask the Martians to settle down in the observatory emergency quarters and help them in any way we can,' Brown said briskly.

Watson and the others murmured in agreement, so Brown said to Jim, 'It's all right, we'll keep the Martians, but trust me, it will be a hard job. So long, good night.' At that moment, the translator blurted out: 'First we'll have to get converted into simple human beings to survive, and secondly, destroy the ship in which we came or Maradonio will not take long to come to Earth to kill us, or worse, punish us!'

The scientists' team considered the matter.

'We'll be dead within an hour if we don't get a shot of the current DNA of humans adapted to the earth's habitat, or if our ship isn't destroyed. Maradonio will come and destroy Earth if he wants. But he can trace us only if he can catch the radio waves our ship emits.' The Martians showed them proof of this on the screen in the hall.

Brown said in a concluding sort of way, 'Call Mr Hemming, he can use our super universal biological conversion device to change these poor Martians' biology! Watson call Hemming now, we have no time to waste. Jim confirmed that these creatures are playing no joke. Their body outline is getting fainter every minute. Now George and Evans you can examine this ship; find out what kind of waves it emits. Larry you can turn on the biochemical converter that was constructed with so much of painstaking hard work.'

At that moment, Watson stormed in from the call room. 'Hemming's a hero! He is already examining the biology of one of the creatures in the emergency room. The Martian says that they have an odd power. If one of them is successfully converted into a human, the others will automatically be converted when the creature touches the others. So the work can be done easily after one conversion.'

All the scientists marched up to the emergency room while the rest of the Martians retreated to their ship.

Hemming was perspiring. 'Peculiar structure of genes. Twenty-five pairs of some type of chromosomes that seem charged! It'll be a difficult task! Nerves are absent. There are some types of tubes that transfer the message through magnetic impulses! But wait up, if they are compressed and hard X-rays are passed through the genes, then they'll lose their charge and then I can easily use a living human gene to co-ordinate with the Martians' cells. The only problem is how to link the two cells without destroying chromosomes that may cause their death!' said Hemming, doing a number of things at the same time.

In the end, Hemming had a brainwave. He displaced three of the chromosomes of the Martian living cell, with three chromosomes from human cells, which of course co-ordinated, because the Martian cell was actually a human cell. Hemming chained this procedure through a malignant but controlled cell division and eliminated the rest of the Martian cells.

An astonishing effect followed. The Martian creature slowly developed a head, then the extra hands were sucked inwards. A gurgling noise filled the containers in which the Martian was kept.

'Get out of the room he's gonna explode!' someone shouted. Everyone tumbled pell-mell out of the room. The said explosion took place with the sound of the breaking of many test tubes.

Hemming gingerly walked back into the room with Watson and the others. On one end of the room, there lay a small baby fast asleep in the container in which the Martian had been.

The rest of the Martians came into the room. One by one they touched the baby. Without any explosion they were converted into human beings. Hemming used an extra injection of activated simple DNA-1 solution to quicken the growth rate of the Martians-turned-babies.

Meanwhile, George and Evans had found out the frequency and wavelength of the radio waves emitted by the pyramidal ship. The radio waves were unstoppable as they were produced by a strong electric field in the ship.

'If we want to neutralise the field, we'll have to use the Hardener's law machine. That will probably destroy the ship as well as the observatory,' said Evans. But seeing the shocked look on Brown's face, he hastily added, 'There's another technique, but it would require the sacrifice of someone's life. If a powerful electromagnetic field is introduced in the electric field it can neutralise the latter if high energy microwaves are emitted from one end. However, someone can get trapped in either field if the right timing isn't maintained. We have to introduce the magnet, activate the particle accelerator and quickly hop out of the twenty-feet high door of the ship, before the radio waves, microwaves and electromagnetic field waves can interact.'

'I'll do it,' said Brown, with a determined look, 'before the Martian king can come to Earth.'

'Okay, get on, I've already set the magnet in position inside the pyramid. Just turn it on, turn on the accelerator and get on!'

Brown's partners closed their eyes and ears, ready for anything to happen. After an hour's wait they heard an explosion, saw the pyramid exploding, and Brown jumping out. There were yells, cheers, greetings …

'And we legally accept the Martians as American citizens on Earth. We award Mr Brown and Mr Max Watson bravery awards for their unparalleled courage,' the UNO president announced in their Assembly a week later.

Shriya Pilgaonkar

Shriya Pilgaonkar, sixteen-years old, is from Utpal Shanghvi School, Mumbai, the most happening city in India.

She has found her own world within the hustle and bustle of the city. She believes that when you really want something the entire universe conspires to get it for you. She has varied interests ranging from sports to singing and from dancing to music. She loves learning foreign languages and is currently working on her Japanese. She also likes reading and writing poetry and wants to be known for what she writes. Shriya loves teaching and would like to teach underprivileged children but is undecided about her career and believes in going with the flow of life.

Every time she writes, she learns something new about herself and she sees writing as a means of self communication. Her favourite authors are Roald Dahl, Ruskin Bond, Agatha Christie and a few of her favourite books are *The Alchemist* by Paulo Coelho, *Mr God this is Anna* by Fynn, *To kill a Mocking Bird* by Harper Lee and *Jonathan Livingston Seagull* by Richard Bach. A quote which she really identifies with is 'I must create a system or else be enslaved by another man's. I will not reason and compare. My business is to create' by William Blake.

She was awarded the Jury Special Mention award for her authorship.

AN APPOINTMENT WITH GOD

Shriya Pilgaonkar (Mumbai)

In the throes of pain, the woman screamed a cry of sheer anguish! Echoes bounced off the walls and a sudden cold wave fell over the world. She was yelling in pain, a pain which had gripped her trembling body like a leech. But alas! Everyone was indifferent to her plight.

Satish woke up with a start! He could feel cold sweat, slowly tricking down his face. He had had enough!

It was Christmas Eve and the people of Shimla were blessed with a white Christmas. Satish lay on his bed, still as a pillar. He was an innocent, eight-year-old boy who had recently been haunted by some very strange, but funny nightmares. Strange because he had never seen any of those horrific sights before, and funny because he had no clue as to who those people were, who gave him sleepless nights. What did they want from him?

Satish got up from his bed and stumbled over a pillow. He figured that he must have been throwing things around all night. It was still dark outside and he could see the narrow streets covered with the whitest and softest snow ever. He glanced at his watch. It was five-thirty. Satish, who was now calmer than before, sat on his favourite armchair. It was like his stress-buster. The comfortable pillows and armrest made him feel as if he was being hugged by a person from behind. It had been a couple of nights now that Satish had been dreaming of people in pain, terror and terribly devastated. He wondered why he dreamt about such frightening things. He had never gone through any turmoil as a child and had always been blessed with a serene, peaceful environment. Shimla didn't have much of a dark side to talk about. It was as if nothing could ever go wrong in this little town.

But Satish, who was a very sensitive boy, was very intimidated by the happenings all around the world. He read about people being killed, murdered, and isolated. He wondered how he was living a happy and blissful life, when the world outside was being shattered by the day. Satish suddenly opened his eyes, after being immersed in deep thought, and to his surprise, he saw a red stocking hanging on the wall. How could he have forgotten that it was Christmas? The next day? He smiled and got the stocking, hung on a nail. Every year, on Christmas, Satish had a gala time. Gifts, chocolates and a Christmas tree. 'I am too old for stockings and presents and ...' he thought, but suddenly realised that he wasn't too old for Santa! It was like a ritual. Every year Satish would make a list of all the things that he desired for Christmas and would pleasantly receive them the next day. Last year he had asked for a cycle and boy, was he happy when he saw the Hercules cycle in the backyard. But this time, Satish wanted something different. He had to take advantage of the fact that he was writing to Santa, who was popular for fulfilling any and every wish that children had. Still in his pyjamas and very sleepy, he picked up his notebook and scribbled on it—An Appointment with God. He had too much to ask God and more than ever, too much to say. Satish wanted to make the world a better place, and although he had no reason to worry or care about the world outside, he knew somewhere in his heart that he was born to do good.

Grandfather was stunned. 'An appointment with God? This is completely an oh-my-God situation! We ask a little eight-year-old boy to ask Santa for a gift, maybe a pair of skates or a book. But Satish asks for an appointment to meet God!' exclaimed grandpa. Satish's father, who was reading the newspaper, glanced up and smiled at him. 'Satish is smart, don't you think?' Satish had placed his scrap of paper into the stocking the night before, wanting to have his wish fulfilled. He assumed that Santa and God were close pals. No wonder that Santa knew whenever he was well-behaved or when he was a naughty boy. God must have told him every year. Grandpa, along with Satish's father, were in a fix. They would never be able to fix an appointment with God!

Satish got up from his sleep and lazily entered the living room. 'Good morning. Has it being snowing all night?' he asked, rubbing his eyes and peeping through the window. 'Yes. Wonderful, isn't it?' said his father. 'Satish, what shall we do for Christmas? Want to go shopping?' 'I don't feel like it papa,' said Satish and dropped himself on the couch. He felt very grumpy this morning and even the wintry morning failed to bring some cheer in his heart. He was too upset. Satish was a boy who could easily be affected. The mind of a child is like clay; it takes the shape it is moulded into and Satish was very affected by the fact that people were suffering. He always did his best to help people. He had recently befriended a blind boy, George, who studied at the Shimla School for the Blind. Satish found Brail to be very fascinating, and George had taught it to him.

Meanwhile, grandpa was wondering how he should fix an appointment with God. He certainly couldn't dress as God. He would be cursed for the rest of his life if he did that! Grandpa chuckled at the thought of it. He loved Satish dearly and shared a very special bond with him. No one knew Satish better than he did. He knew how much his grandson felt for people and cared for the sick. In a modern world, when human bonds were slowly breaking, and people were living in a sea of loneliness, this little boy wanted to reach out to people living in bleak, dark homes. Grandfather decided to have a little talk with Satish.

It was eight-thirty in the evening and the world seemed to be ready for Christmas. The shops and streets had the same theme: Santa Claus and the colour red. Satish had spent the day with his father reading. He loved the way in which his father read out to him. They had had some lovely story-telling sessions before, too. This time, the story was about angels and fairies and the good and the bad. Satish enjoyed the way in which his father enacted every emotion with dexterity. Satish was in his room, cleaning it. He did not want God to come and see the mess as his next Christmas gift was at stake. He jumped up and got into his pyjamas. He felt anxious and very excited. Just then, grandfather entered. He had toyed with various ideas before getting this one. 'Satish, let's have some fun. Why don't you close your eyes and sit on your chair for some time,' said grandpa. Satish ran to his favourite armchair and plopped into it.

'Close your eyes, Satish, and listen and imagine. You are standing on a mountain, right at the top. It is as if you have reached the zenith of success or of life. You are surrounded by clouds. They keep coming in your way and everything seems to be a haze to you. You peer down and see a small village. A boy is waving at you. He is calling out to you. Go to him Satish. Slide down the mountain slope with the wind blowing on your face. The cold is pricking your little hands.' Satish could feel the lurch of the mountains, the untresspassed sanctity of space and the proximity of God. Satish was now standing at the base of the mountain. He was alone. Suddenly, he heard the rustling of leaves. 'Leaves? There are no leaves on the trees right now,' thought Satish. He then heard a voice, a strong, piercing voice. 'Talk to me Satish, you wanted to meet me, didn't you?' 'Is that you

Mister God?' asked Satish excitedly. 'Why are so many people unhappy? Why do little boys cry? Why are we in pain, even though you protect us?' he started, asking too many questions even before the voice could confirm its presence. 'Satish, listen to me. I gave man the world, a place to call his own. He did what he could to nourish this holy land and prayed and prayed till all his desires were fulfilled. Later, he gradually started focusing his attention on himself. He wanted everything for himself. I had no place in his heart, which became so cold and lifeless. Money gave him his power and his authority. I could not help him anymore.' 'But doesn't it hurt you that your children are suffering? You must give them another chance. You can make a difference. I can't!' There was laughter in the air, and the voice said, 'That is where you are wrong, my child. Only man understands man. If I give you all the happiness and take away all the sorrow in a jiffy, sorrow will not vanish forever. Man has not realised his soul's purpose of living.' 'Why do you let all the good people die? If you keep them alive, they can make the world a better place,' protested Satish timidly. 'My son let me tell you a secret. I have allotted duties to each and every soul on this earth. The day the duty is performed and completed, the person comes up to my abode, where I give him a gift for the good job that he did whilst he was on earth.'

The voice rang in Satish's ears. 'God, what I can do to help? My friends say that you don't exist. Will you tell them all what you told me?' 'Satish, a person who does not believe in me has no one to thank when he is truly thankful. Remember this.' Satish was about to ask the voice something when the sky shot open and the rustling leaves rose in the air. They shot up towards the sky and slowly and steadily, the sky opened and the sun's rays emerged like the embalming hand of God. They fell on Satish, who stood there completely mesmerised. The bright sunray pierced his eyes and he covered them for safety; the light was too strong for him to keep his eyes open. He shut them tightly with all his might, avoiding every speck of dust that swirled around him. Then all of a sudden, the noise died down. Satish opened his eyes and there he was, lying on his bed with grandfather staring right into his eyes.

'Merry Christmas Satish! Wake up. It's morning. Don't you want to open the presents? Come on you lazy boy, get up, it's Christmas!' Satish did not remember doing anything on that day. It was the most beautiful Christmas day and yet he felt burdened. As stepped out of the house to go for a walk, he saw a pile of leaves in the corner. He smiled because he knew that he did have an appointment with God in reality. He understood that he could make a difference and believed that he was given a chance to live, just so that he could make this world a better place.

EPILOGUE

Satish grew up to be a Noble Prize winner and kept his promise. He often thought about his childhood and how it had inspired him to reach such heights and develop a penchant for social service.

Recently, when asked in an interview about the most wonderful moment of his life, Satish replied without any hesitation, 'My appointment with God.'

Sreerupa Chowdhury

For this fifteen-year-old girl from Mahadevi Birla Girls' Higher Secondary School, Kolkata, writing is a passion. 'It's my solitary refuge amidst chaos and my best friend', says Sreerupa Chowdhury. 'Through my story, "News at 09:00", I've made an attempt at understanding some of the many complexities of the human psyche—fear, guilt and conflict.' While reading and writing are next to breathing for Sreerupa, 'debates, quizzes, singing, dancing, laughing and reinventing myself by being creative are my other passions. I also suffer from a disease —"verbal diarrhoea!"' Challenges, 'FRIENDS' (the TV sitcom and also those in real life), Harry Potter and learning new stuff invigorate Sreerupa. Her self-written quip on life is: 'Life is worth its weight in dreams.' Her favourite book is *Gone with the Wind* by Margaret Mitchell. P.G. Wodehouse, William Shirer, Frederick Forsyth and O'Henry are her favourite authors.

She was awarded the second runner-up position in the contest.

THE NEWS AT 9:00

SREERUPA CHOWDHURY (KOLKATA)

'... And now, for the last piece of news for the day. This is to alert all residents of New Jalpaiguri that a woman killer is amongst their midst, and their lives are in grave danger. Apparently, this killer strikes at random—her victims are chosen on the spur of the moment. Police reports indicate that so far six lives have been claimed by her, including one infant and a two-year-old child. She has never been caught in the actual act and has successfully evaded all attempts to track her down. It is only by virtue of a thorough investigation led by Chief Superintendent J.P. Saigal that the police have managed to ascertain that there is a woman's hand behind all these seemingly unrelated heinous crimes. All six victims were residents of New Jalpaiguri. She has no fixed modus operandi, her—' Maya switched off the television set, unwilling to hear any more. With a start she realised she was sweating profusely, even with the air conditioner on. Her breath was coming out fast and shallow even as she felt an unbearable tightening in her chest. For the first time in her life, Maya Chatterjee was afraid.

It all began two days ago. Maya had been on her way to the local bazaar to get her weekly supply of groceries, when all of a sudden, she had an inexplicable feeling that someone was watching her. She spun around, but found the street deserted, except for a few children playing by the roadside. Shaking off her stupid fears, she had plodded on, but the eerie feeling had still persisted. 'I am too stressed out,' she reasoned. 'It has been this way since Rajiv's death. I should probably go on a vacation. Somewhere like ... Mauritius, or closer home, say Goa. A long, well-deserved holiday on the beach, revelling in the sheer joy of being alive....' She was lost in her dreams. But at the back of her mind, was a nagging doubt, that perhaps things weren't as simple as she was trying to make herself believe. Maybe a holiday wasn't exactly the panacea to her problems. Maybe ... maybe she was imagining all of it. She willed herself to stay positive. 'Rajiv, I wish you were here,' she thought. 'If only things had worked out.'

Rajiv had been her husband, her companion, her life. Their three years of marital life had passed like a dream until—until the other woman had wrenched him away from her. The other woman had seized what belonged to her—

her most precious Rajiv. Even Maya's steely nerves and determination had crumbled to dust during the harrowing separation. Rajiv had left her his ancestral house in Jalpaiguri as alimony and had left for Kolkata to start afresh. Even though she had tried, she could never bring herself to hate Rajiv for what he had done. Instead, she was filled with a deep hatred and jealousy for the woman who usurped her happiness.

A slight rap on the windowpane made her come out of her stupor. She glanced at the clock on the mantelpiece. Nine-thirty in the evening, and already it felt like the stillness of midnight had descended all around. The nine o'clock news had left her devastated. Her worst apprehensions had been confirmed. For two days Maya had felt the presence of this anonymous adversary, biding her time, poised to strike. And now, she knew that it hadn't been a product of her overactive imagination. Her fears were genuine.

Maya suddenly realised what this implied and looking around at the emptiness around her, knew how vulnerable she must be. Her antagonist might be near her this very moment, laughing at her loneliness. In a fit of desperation, Maya rushed to the French windows of the palatial mansion and started banging them shut. The echoes of the clanging windowpanes filled the silence of the night. Maya was shivering uncontrollably by this time. She realised what a fool she had been to have misinterpreted the warning signals of her subconscious. Maya suddenly froze in her tracks. She had left the kitchen door, adjoining her backyard garden, open. That meant the killer could be lurking inside the house.

At the very moment when this blood-curdling thought occurred to her, Maya heard the unmistakable sounds of muffled footsteps, as if someone was walking very stealthily in order to avoid detection. Maya lived alone. So, either one of Maya's friends had decided to pay Maya a rare surprise visit at this late hour, or the psychotic killer was inside the house that very moment having her nocturnal stroll. The latter option being more plausible, Maya reacted as any normal individual would—she screamed.

Her howls reverberated about the walls of the mansion, and the echoes seemed to be the cruel mocking of the unforgiving darkness. Outside the night air hung heavy with fog, inside it was dense with tremors of evil.

Now, Maya's only chance of escape was getting help from outside, though there was a slim chance of this as well, there being no human life in the immediate vicinity. The nearest apartment was two kilometres away. Near Maya's residence was a lonely stretch of road, it's only characteristic being just that—lonely.

Even though it was hopeless, Maya blindly stumbled across the living room, wrenched open the door and made her way outside. As can be expected in a small-town junction like New Jalpaiguri, the street lights had long ceased functioning. Maya inched ahead, careful to keep to the shadows as much as possible. This at least was not difficult, since the filtered light from the mansion didn't exactly obliterate the darkness outside.

She was hunched behind one of the bushes when Maya sensed movement behind her. She could not move; her legs seemed to be paralysed with fear. Her adversary had found her at last; her feelings of relief were now ebbing away. But she wouldn't surrender, not this easily. She wouldn't accept defeat even if it meant fighting till her last breath. Even with Rajiv, she hadn't given up. Rajiv ... she sternly banished thoughts about him from her mind. She was in a crisis, she reminded herself.... Slowly, she wheeled around, willing herself to face her nemesis.

She stared in horror. The face staring back at her was her own mirror image. Except for the fact that there was blood dripping from her eyes, and her mouth was twisted in a cruel sneer. Her alter ego was clutching a dagger in one hand. It was the same woman who had taken Rajiv away from her. This woman was responsible for everything that had gone wrong in her life. This woman had murdered her beloved Rajiv and left her a widow. She was evil, and Maya knew it. She must finish off this woman before she caused any more harm. Maya picked up a slab of stone lying near her feet, and with all her strength, hurled it across, hitting the woman on the head, until blood oozed out. There was a blinding pain in her forehead, but she ignored it, determined to make the 'evil' suffer as much she had suffered all this while. She kept hitting the slab on the woman's head, till she realised blood was soaking through her own hair and spilling on to her clothes. Her alter ego was disappearing ... or was it just her vision getting blurred? Maya couldn't tell for certain, because her brain had stopped working. The last thing she saw before falling unconscious to the ground was Rajiv's handsome face, smiling down benignly at her. But that couldn't be could it, because Rajiv was dead.

'... Ladies and gentlemen, what a dramatic story this has been. A jealous wife, driven to madness by her obsession with her husband, murders him in cold blood when he falls in love with his secretary. The wife, Maya Chatterjee, was so overwhelmed with guilt that she created another character, possibly modelled on the secretary, on whom she could squarely rest the blame, and thus relieve her conscience. To make this concept of "the other woman" more plausible, she murdered six innocent residents of New Jalpaiguri, just to prove the existence of this woman, who in reality was a figment of her imagination. But her guilt and her all-consuming love for her husband gave her no peace. So in her twisted reasoning, she decided to settle all scores with her hated nemesis. The consequences of this rendezvous you are all aware of. What actually happened last night, why she caused her own destruction, perhaps we shall never be able to comprehend. But on the basis of what Mr Ram Sachdev, who was passing by her mansion yesterday, observed, the police have come to the conclusion that Mrs Maya Chatterjee hit herself with a stone slab several times, which caused severe haemorrhaging. Mr Sachdev rushed her to the nearest hospital as fast as possible, where she breathed her last this morning. The doctor declared death due to injuries sustained. The police, along with eminent psychiatrists, have been able to reconstruct the sad episodes which led to this startling climax from snatches of what she said in hospital last night.

Thus ends the remarkable story of love, passion, betrayal, murder, repentance and, finally, retribution.' With that the news at 9:00 concluded.